DEDICATED TO: NATE, MAC & SUNNY.
ALSO TO EZRA, PORTER & KEIGHTLEY.
READ THIS WHEN YOU CAN'T SLEEP.
-XOXO

CROISSANT AND MOLASSES

THIS IS MOLASSES

MOLASSES IS GROSS.

DOG IN GLASSES

CAN YOU GUESS HIS
NAME?

COWBOY BOOTS

PERFECT FOR ROPING
& RIDING!

RANDOM FRUITS

 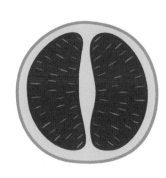 

DOES IT COUNT IF
IT'S BAKED INTO A
PIE?

TALKING CAT

BIRTHDAY HAT

TECHNICALLY ANY HAT CAN BE
A BIRTHDAY HAT WHEN YOU
WEAR IT ON YOUR BIRTHDAY.

LITTLE HOUSE

THIS HOUSE IS IN
ROCKDALE, TX.

CITY MOUSE

HE NORMALLY TAKES
THE SUBWAY.

HOT AIR BALOON

WAIT. HOW'D HE
GET IN THERE?

KING RACCOON

TONIGHT I FEAST.

CUP OF TEA

DOESN'T READING
MAKE YOU THIRSTY?

BOAT AT SEA

I WRITE WITH MY
STARBOARD HAND.

FANCY PANTS

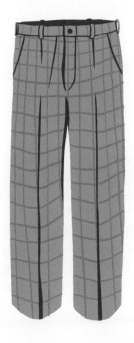

EXACTLY LIKE
REGULAR PANTS BUT
FANCIER.

SOMEWHERE IN FRANCE

WE SHOULD GO THERE
SOMEDAY.

COZY SWEATER

SO. COZY.

UNREAD LETTER

WONDER WHAT IT SAYS..

HOUSE PLANT

YOU DON'T HAVE TO
REMEMBER TO WATER
THIS ONE.

GIANT ANT

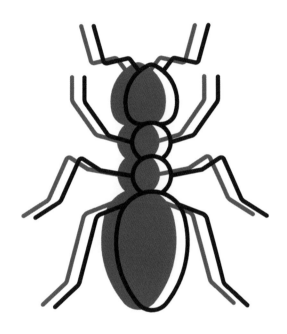

UNFORTUNATELY THESE
EXIST.

TUCK IN TIGHT

DON'T WIGGLE OR
YOU'LL UNTUCK
YOURSELF!

SAY GOODNIGHT

(THIS IS THE PART WHERE YOU GO TO
SLEEP.)

ABOUT THE AUTHOR

TAYLOR JOHNSTON

TAYLOR LIVES ON A GOAT FARM IN
THE HEARTLAND WITH HER HUSBAND
& THREE KIDS. SHE LOVES DRINKING
COFFEE & STARTING PROJECTS. SHE
ALSO DAYDREAMS A LOT. IT'S NOT THE
BEST COMBINATION BUT SHE'S
LEARNED TO PLAY THE HAND SHE'S
BEEN DEALT.

Printed in Great Britain
by Amazon

22966497R10016